IGGY

M.G. HIGGINS

SAD
EDUCA

D1113253

WHITE LIGHTNING
BOOKS

BREAK AND ENTER

IGGY

ON THE RUN

QWIK CUTTER

REBEL

SCRATCH N' SNITCH

SADDLEBACK
EDUCATIONAL PUBLISHING
www.sdlback.com

ISBN-13: 978-1-68021-111-5
ISBN-10: 1-68021-111-0
eBook: 978-1-63078-428-7

NOV 0 9 2016

Printed in Guangzhou, China
NOR/1015/CA21501554

20 19 18 17 16   1 2 3 4 5

DIFFERENCES BETWEEN PORTLAND AND LAS VEGAS

#1 DONUT SHOPS (BASED ON YELP REVIEWS)

PORTLAND
VOODOO DOUGHNUTS

LAS VEGAS
RONALD'S DONUTS

PORTLAND   POPULATION 619,000

LAS VEGAS   POPULATION 613,000

TOURISM

PORTLAND
8.6 MILLION

LAS VEGAS
41 MILLION

I HOPE I DON'T MEET ONE OF THESE!

CHAPTER 1

COYOTE AVENUE

The plane jerks. I open my eyes. "Ignacia Suarez?"

The flight attendant smiles down at me. So does the jolly plastic Santa pin on her collar. "We'll be landing in Las Vegas in ten minutes. Stay on the plane until everyone else is off. Then someone from the airline will meet you. They'll take you to baggage claim. Okay?"

"Okay," I answer.

She continues up the aisle, collecting trash.

I sit up straight. Look out the window. The ground is flat and brown. So different from Oregon. I wish Dad hadn't moved so far away. And to Nevada of all places.

"I'm sure you and your stepmom will get along fine," says the woman sitting next to me. I'd told her why I'm flying alone. I'm spending winter break with my dad and new stepmom.

I let out a shaky breath. "I hope so."

"Remember, she's as nervous to meet you as you are to meet her. I'm sure they've got your holiday all planned out. You're going to have a great time."

I hope she's right. "What were those places you said before? The fun things to do?"

"Well, let's see," she says. "There's the Big Apple Coaster. Adventuredome. The Big Shot ride. Adventure Canyon. Your parents will know where to go."

It sounds like fun and makes me feel a little

better. Maybe this won't be such a terrible winter
break after all.

"Iggy!" Dad waves from baggage claim. He
looks a little heavier. But otherwise the same.
Five foot seven. Pizza-crust-colored skin. Thick
black hair.

"Hi, Dad."

He lifts me off the ground. Grips me in a bear
hug. "It's so good to see you. I can't believe it's
been over a year."

"Yeah." He feels good. Smells good too. Lime
aftershave, just like I remember.

I wish he didn't have to set me down. But he
does. Now I'm face-to-face with Tiffany. Dad sent
me pictures. But seeing her is still kind of a shock.
She's tall. Thin. Blonde. The complete opposite of
my dad. Opposite of everyone in my family.

Tiffany is wearing a stiff white shirt. Her hair
poofs out like a blonde helmet. The only parts of

her body not at attention are her eyes. They sag at the ends. It's like she's already tired of me.

"Hello, Iggy. It's nice to meet you." She sticks her hand out.

"Hi." I shake her bony fingers.

"Your father has told me so much about you."

I have no idea what to say. *It's not nice to meet you. You should have left my dad alone. Given him time to get back with Mom.* I don't say anything.

Dad clears his throat. Takes my suitcase. "Okay. Let's go."

We drive forever on a freeway. Then another freeway. Then down lots of streets that all look alike. We pass houses that all look alike. Dad turns up Coyote Avenue and pulls into the driveway of a white house. The front yard has one skinny tree. Four spiny cactuses. And a lawn of bright white rocks instead of grass.

"We're here," he says proudly.

I follow them inside. Go through a white living

room. Down a white hallway. Into a white bedroom where Dad sets down my suitcase. "We really want you to feel at home here. Don't we, Tiff?"

"Of course," Tiffany says softly.

Dad gives me another hug. "I'm so glad you're here. Make yourself at home. I have a little work to do." He winks and leaves.

Tiffany smiles awkwardly. Pats my arm the way you'd pat a baby's back to get the burps out. "Go ahead and put your things away. The bathroom's down the hall. Let me know if you need anything." She skips out of there like bees are chasing her.

I call Mom's phone. Get her voice mail. "I'm here."

Then I text my best friend, Sophia.

IGGY: Merry Saturday before Xmas from Las Vegas!

I look around the super-neat room. Just a bed, a dresser, and a desk. Nothing out of place. My bedroom in Oregon has yellow walls. A purple bedspread. I haven't seen the top of my desk since I was three. Which is exactly the way I like it.

This is an alien planet.

I need to get out of here.

CHAPTER 2

CREEP-O-METER

I wander down the hallway. Hear Dad talking on the phone. "Yes, I understand." Pause. "You'll have it Monday." He hangs up.

I peek around the doorway. This must be his office. "Dad?"

He jerks his head up. "Oh, hi, sweetie."

"I thought maybe we could go into town."

"Town?"

"I hear the Adventuredome is cool. Or maybe one of those roller coasters?"

"You want to go to the Strip?" He laughs like I told a funny joke. Then he sees I'm not smiling. "You just got here. Anyway, I have to go to work."

"It's Saturday."

"I know. I'm sorry, Iggy. The timing it terrible. But this is a big new client, and I have to impress them. How about we take a walk tomorrow? We'll go to the park. I know you love to swing."

"When I was five."

I don't think he heard me. He throws papers into a briefcase. Crosses the room and kisses my forehead. "See you later. Have fun."

Fun? Right.

I wander through the bright boring house. Find my way to the kitchen. Tiffany's chopping something at a gleaming white countertop. She twists around.

"Oh. Hi. You can take a nap if you like. You must be tired."

"I can't sleep. It's too bright. What's with all the white?"

"White goes with everything."

"So does flaming sunset yellow. I saw a Home Depot when we drove in. They have lots of paint."

Her smile wavers. She turns back to her cutting board.

I tap the counter. "Do you mind if I go for a walk?"

She squints. "Really? Now? I haven't discussed this with your father."

I sigh. "It's just a walk."

"Do you have your cell phone?"

I nod.

She lets out a long breath. "All right. But don't go any farther than our neighborhood. One square block. Okay?"

"Fine."

I pass a rock lawn with a herd of plastic reindeer.

Another rock lawn with three little elves and a deflated snowman. Poor Frosty. No wonder he's melting. I can't believe Christmas is five days away. It's nearly seventy degrees.

I reach the end of the block. There's a sign on the corner. An arrow is pointing in a direction Tiffany told me not to go. It says Harrison Park.

Hmmm.

I cross the street. Reach the park three blocks later. The trees are surprisingly big. As if the park has been here for a while. There's a playground with swings. It's empty. No screaming kids around. What the heck? I'm not five anymore. But I don't have anything better to do.

I get on a swing. Kick off. Go as high as I can. I love the feeling of wind blowing against my face. Like I'm flying. The air is fresh. Not after-the-rain fresh like in Portland. But a dry fresh. Like the first Oreo out of a box.

I finally get tired. Let the swing slow to a stop.

"Happy holidays!"

I look over. A kid is sitting on one of the swings.

"Do you go to Jefferson?" he asks.

"No."

"I didn't think so. I've never seen you at school. Where are you from?"

"Portland."

"Oregon?"

"Yeah."

"There's also a Portland, Maine, you know. Your Portland gets about forty inches of rain a year. A lot more interesting weather than here. Do you mind if I sit closer? That way I won't have to yell."

My creep-o-meter is dinging. But he asked politely. And he's kind of cute. "Okay."

He leaps off. He walks with a limp. Sits on the swing next to mine. I think he's about my age. His eyes are green. His sandy-brown hair could use some styling, but it's nicely mussed.

"Why are you limping?" I ask. "Did you hurt your leg?"

"No, I was born this way." He smiles, dimples forming in his cheeks.

It's like he was just hoping I'd ask this question.

"Limb Length Discrepancy. Also called Short Leg Syndrome. I was in an awkward position in my mother's womb before I was born. It didn't develop right. I usually wear an orthotic to make my legs even. But I grew out of my old one. The new one won't be ready for a couple of weeks. Mom says it wasn't entirely my fault I got twisted around. She did power yoga during her pregnancy with me. She switched to Pilates before she had my sister." He stops talking. "Sorry. Is that too much information?"

"Um, yeah. A bit."

"Sorry. Sometimes I talk a lot."

He may be cute, but my creep-o-meter is now screeching. And Tiffany must be wondering why my walk around the block is taking so long. "I have to go." I jump off my swing.

"My name is Lucas. I'm usually here in the afternoons."

"Okay. Well, see ya."

He smiles and waves. "See ya!"

Right. That's not going to happen.

CHAPTER 3

THE MALL

Dad ends up working most of Sunday too. So we don't go to the park. Then it's Monday. A workday. He's gone before I get up.

This is ridiculous. We're fifteen miles from one of the most exciting cities in the world. And I might spend my entire vacation reading and watching TV. That lady on the plane was so wrong. My parents do *not* have a fun holiday all planned out for me.

I run into Tiffany in the hallway. She jerks

back when she sees me. Like I have cooties. As if she's not swarming with them herself. But she may be my only hope for salvaging this vacation.

"You doing anything today?" I ask.

"I have some work to finish." She writes verses for greeting cards. "What did you have in mind?"

"Can we go to the Strip?"

Her face pales. "No, of course not. It's too far. Too many people."

I roll my eyes. "What about the mall?"

"The mall? Why?"

"Because it's something to do! Listen to holiday music. Look at decorations. You know?"

"But the mall is so crowded. And we have decorations." She flutters her spidery fingers around. Toward the fake tree and metal reindeer in the living room.

I let out a sigh.

"I'm sorry, Iggy," she says. "I don't …" She covers her eyes with her hand. Then she sucks in a deep breath. "Okay. Sure. There's a present I still need to buy. Let's go to the mall."

Tiffany starts her Subaru wagon. Backs slowly out of the driveway. Maybe she's afraid she'll run over something. She drives down Coyote Avenue at ten miles an hour.

I tap my knees. "Mind if I turn on the radio?"

"Go ahead."

I find a pop station.

"So who's your favorite singer?" she asks.

"You're too old. You wouldn't know anything about the kind of music I like. Why even ask?"

She sighs. "Iggy, I know you're upset. Your parents aren't together anymore. But I didn't steal your father. They were separated when we met."

"I know."

"So how do I make you like me?"

I didn't even know she was trying.

She slams the breaks suddenly. The car jerks to a stop. "Shoot," she mutters.

There's a line of cars. It's two blocks long. They're waiting to get into the mall parking lot.

"It's going to be a long wait," she says.

"I don't mind." Waiting gives me time. I mentally outline my mall-shopping game plan. First the Pretzel Palace. Because I'll need to carbo-load for lots of walking. I'll definitely visit Jean Junction. And Sindrella's for hoodies. Pete's Pets to look at puppies.

It's five minutes later. Tiffany croaks, "We've barely moved."

"Well, yeah. It's three days before Christmas. What did you expect?"

"I don't know." Her voice cracks. It looks like she's about to cry. Her knuckles turn white on the steering wheel. What is wrong with her?

"What do you need to buy?" I ask.

"Um … just a little something for your father. A stocking stuffer."

"You mean like a pen? Something you can get at a drugstore?"

She nods.

Clearly she'd rather do something else. Like sit naked on an iceberg. I'm glad she can't hear my mean thoughts. "Pull out. When the guy ahead of us moves foward."

She glances at me. "You mean leave? Are you sure?"

"Yeah."

"Well. Only if you're sure."

"I'm sure!"

She pulls out of the line of cars like a NASCAR driver.

She buys Dad a present. One of those screwdriver-jackknife things at Walgreen's.

"Your dad isn't very handy around the house," she says at the checkout counter. "Maybe this will inspire him." She smiles. The color back in her cheeks. But there's still a droopy tiredness in her eyes.

Am I that exhausting?

Probably.

Does she want to be my stepmom?

No way.

CHAPTER 4

NORMAL FAMILY

Dad stops chewing his toast. Stares at me. Like I've just told him I want to visit Afghanistan. "No, Iggy. I'm working. And the Strip is really busy on holidays."

I push my plate away. "You guys are so boring."

"Are you sure you didn't bring any homework?" he asks.

"Yes!"

"I just read an article in the newspaper,"

Tiffany says. "There's a holiday reading program. It's at the library."

"The *library*?"

"Iggy. She's just trying to help." Dad gets up from the table. Pats my shoulder. Kisses the top of my head. "I'm sorry you're disappointed. I have a vacation day after Christmas. We'll do something special then. All right?"

"Fine."

Dad and Tiffany share a kiss. I try to keep from throwing up. His skin color is several shades darker than hers. She's two inches taller. But they somehow fit together. Tiff-Daddy.

I need to go for a walk.

That kid, Lucas, said he only uses the swings in the afternoons. So I should be safe. But I bypass the playground. Use a different entrance. Just in case. I walk down a dirt path. It winds its way through a bunch of trees. Ends at a few picnic tables. One of them is occupied. The occupier looks up from his book when he sees me. "Oh, hi!"

Dang.

"Are you lost?" he asks.

"Nope. Just going for a walk. Looking at the trees."

"Oh, cool! Do you want to be a dendrologist?"

"A what?"

"A scientist who studies trees."

"Uh, no. I just like looking at them."

"I thought I wanted to be a dendrologist for a while. But I like meteorology better."

"I don't know much about meteors."

"Meteorology is the science of weather."

"Oh. Right." I turn to leave.

"You never told me your name," he says.

I think about not telling him. But what's he going to do? Steal my identity? "Iggy."

"Is that short for Ignacia?"

"Yeah. It is." No one ever guesses my real name.

He nervously fingers the corner of his book. "Do you notice I'm not talking as much as I did Saturday?"

"I don't know. Maybe."

"I'm learning to let other people participate in the conversation. In order to increase my social skills. Friends don't like friends who monopolize conversations." He opens his mouth to say something. Clamps it shut.

"What?" I ask.

"It's your turn to talk."

"But I don't have anything to say."

He takes a deep breath. Bites his bottom lip.

"What's wrong?" I ask.

"Quiet gaps are very uncomfortable for me."

"They're uncomfortable for most everyone."

He nods. "That's good to know. Do you want to come to my house? It's just down the street. I made an exhibit of cloud formations. It won first place in the county science fair last year."

"No. I should get home."

"Well, maybe another time. Hey, my sister's getting a puppy for Christmas."

"Oh yeah?" I say calmly.

"Christmas Day is too busy. But you could come over the day after. I'll be at the swings at two o'clock."

I shrug. Head back to Coyote Avenue.

I like all animals. But dogs especially. And puppies absolutely. Lucas is a dweeb. But I really want to see his sister's puppy. Except I'm scheduled to go someplace special with my dad. It's a dilemma. But first, I need to get through Christmas.

I've never spent Christmas without Mom. And I haven't spent Christmas with Dad in two years. It's Christmas morning. I sit on the floor. My back is against the side of his easy chair. Like when I was little. I can imagine my mom sitting on the couch instead of Tiffany. If I squint.

Dad picks up the last present. Hands it to me. "Tiffany and I got this for you."

I smile up at him. "Thanks."

He pats my head and laughs. "Do you remember when you believed Santa magically wrapped all your presents with the Christmas paper from the coat closet?"

I snort. "Yeah."

"That's adorable," Tiffany says. "How old were you when you learned Santa wasn't real?"

I drop my jaw. "He's not real?!"

She gives me a stricken look.

"That was a joke," I tell her. "I stopped believing in Santa. I asked for a normal family. Well, he didn't bring one."

"Iggy!" Dad scolds.

Tiffany shrinks farther into the couch.

"Sorry." Wow, I can be such a snot sometimes. I quickly open my present. It's a new smartphone. "Cool. Thanks."

"It's got all the bells and whistles," Dad says. "Very cutting edge."

I tug the bright neon-red phone out of its packaging.

"Do you like the color?" Tiffany asks uncertainly. "That was my contribution."

She didn't choose white? Amazing. "Sure. It's great."

She reaches into her sweater pocket. Pulls out an envelope. Hands it to me. "One last present."

She's already given me a book. ("An award winner!") And a T-shirt. ("I hope it fits!") Now she's giving me something else. I'm a little surprised. I open the envelope. Pull out a greeting card. There's a colored-pencil drawing of an angel on the front. It's homemade. But not tacky. The drawing is really pretty. "Did you make this?" I ask.

She nods.

I slowly open the card. Expect a professional gushy poem. But it's simple.

I'm looking forward to many more holidays with you, Iggy. Love, Tiffany

There's also a gift card. "Home Depot?" I ask in disbelief.

"To buy paint," Tiffany says. "For your room."

"But then the guest room won't match the rest of the house."

"It's not the guest room anymore," she says. "It's *your* room."

"Oh. Well, thanks." I'm sort of impressed. And not sure what else to say. I shove both cards back in the envelope.

Dad presses his hand on my shoulder. "I haven't forgotten my promise. We're doing something special tomorrow."

I doubt driving to the Strip is on his "something special" list. I instantly picture the two of us riding a roller coaster. Of course. Going to some amusement park. That would be worth not seeing the puppy.

CHAPTER 5

DEEPLY NERDY

It's the day after Christmas. Eleven in the morning. Dad still hasn't given me a clue where he's taking me. I've dressed for all possibilities. But mostly for a trip to the Strip. Jeans. The pink "Dad Loves Me Best" T-shirt from Tiffany. (Silly, but it fits.) And sneakers for walking and playing.

I stroll by his office. He's talking on the phone.

"The numbers aren't matching up," he says. He sees me. Holds up his finger. "Uh-huh." Pauses. "Uh-huh. Okay. Sure." He hangs up. Gives me a crooked smile. Gets to his feet. Claps his hands. "How would you like to see where I work?"

What?

"I know this is disappointing. But there's an emergency. It's this new account. I need to spend a couple of hours at the office. If you come with me, we'll at least be together. Then we can catch a movie later."

"I thought we were going to the Strip."

"The Strip? Where did you get that idea?"

"You said someplace special. And I thought maybe—"

"I was going to take you to the Natural History Museum. They've got dinosaurs. You like dinosaurs."

"I'm not eight, Dad."

He sighs. "I'm leaving in a few minutes. I'd like you to come with me. But you don't have to."

I stand in his empty office. Want to run down the street screaming. Kick a few lawn elves. But a *couple hours*? That will at least get me back in time to meet Lucas at the swings. See that puppy. "Dad!" I yell down the hallway. "Are there vending machines where we're going? I really need chocolate!"

Dad's cubicle is a lot messier than his home office. My sixth-grade picture sits in a frame on his desk. Next to a photo of Tiffany. She's wearing a huge smile. She looks happy. No exhausted droop in her eyes.

"Tiffany hates me, doesn't she?"

"Of course she doesn't hate you!" Dad sits on his swivel chair. Turns on his computer.

"Then what's wrong with her?"

"What do you mean?"

"I don't know. She seems fragile or something."

"She's fine. She's just not used to being around kids. But she likes you." He clicks the mouse. "It wouldn't hurt if you were nicer to her."

There's nubby gray carpet lining his cubicle. I drag my fingernails over it. It reminds me of a cat's scratching post. "Did she say that? Does she really like me?"

He reaches into his pocket. Hands me some quarters. "The vending machine is around the corner. There are magazines in the lobby. This will just take two hours. I promise."

I head to the vending machine. Wonder why he didn't answer my question. Probably because Tiffany hates me. Maybe as much as she hates driving to the mall three days before Christmas. She doesn't want to spend more holidays with me. Regardless of what she said in her Christmas card.

The clock on the dashboard reads 2:01. Dad pulls into the driveway.

"Do you mind if I go for a walk?" I ask.

"Really? Now? Well, I guess not. Do you have your new cell phone?"

I pat my pocket.

"Stay in the neighborhood. And be careful. We'll leave for the movie at three thirty."

I break into a run when I'm out of sight. I'm pretty sure Lucas will wait a few minutes. But I don't really know him. Maybe he's lying. Maybe there is no puppy. Maybe he's a juvenile delinquent. Maybe he's planning on robbing me.

He's on a swing. Just where he said he'd be. "Hi," he says with a wave.

I decide to get to the point. "Are you telling the truth about this puppy?"

"I always tell the truth. Honesty is part of the meteorologist's code. The weather is unpredictable. The weatherperson shouldn't be."

I guess I believe him. No one can fake being that deeply nerdy. "Okay. Let's go."

We head down a street. There are old houses and big trees. No rock lawns in sight. Kids race up and down the sidewalks. Toys are scattered across people's front yards. Lucas turns up the brick walkway of a bright blue house.

Oldies rock music blasts from the open front door. A guy is singing. I can tell it's not a recording.

"Who's that?" I ask.

"My dad. You can call him Mr. Elvis."

Mr. Elvis?

CHAPTER 6

MR. ELVIS

Lucas holds the screen door open for me. We step into a living room. A very large man is singing into a microphone. His hair is inky black. His hips swivel. Sweat is pouring down his face. He's singing about being all shaken up. There's lots of *mm-ing. Yeah-ing. Oh-ing.*

It's a little disturbing.

"Dad!" Lucas shouts.

Mr. Elvis sees us and grins. He flips a switch on what I'm guessing is a karaoke machine. The music stops, but my ears keep ringing. "Who is this lovely creature?" he asks.

"This is Iggy," Lucas says.

Mr. Elvis picks up my hand. Like I'm a princess. He stinks. His hand is clammy. But I smile anyway. This is pretty funny. I wish I could snap his photo. Send it to Sophia. She wouldn't believe this.

"Charmed!" He lets go of my hand. "Excuse the clutter. The maid has the day off. Actually, she has the decade off." He laughs at his own joke. "If you'll excuse me, I have to practice. Big gig tonight." He winks. Steps back to the microphone. Flips the switch on the karaoke machine. The room fills again with old rock. His hips swivel.

Lucas whispers in my ear, "He's an Elvis impersonator. In case you haven't figured that out."

"That's his job?"

Lucas shrugs.

"Wow."

Lucas leads me through the house. It really is a mess. Newspapers and magazines scattered across the floors. A dirty bowl sitting on a side table. Tiffany would have a heart attack in here. But it feels comfy and lived-in to me.

I follow Lucas into a bedroom. He closes the door. "Only way to keep the sound out," he explains.

The bass thumps through the wall. But it is quieter. Unlike the rest of the house, the mess in Lucas's room is more controlled. Posters of clouds and tornadoes hang on the walls. He reaches under his bed. Slides out a big piece of cardboard. Holds it up. "This is my award-winning project," he says. "Part of it anyway."

C-U-M-U-L-O-U-S is written in neat block letters across the top. Beneath it are photos of clouds. Drawings of clouds. Cotton-ball sculptures of clouds. Plus charts and diagrams.

"Cool," I say.

"I have four more posters of other cloud types," he says. "And one totally dedicated to hurricanes. Do you want to see them?" He's already reaching under his bed.

There's a knock on the door. A woman with flaming red hair and a very curvy figure walks in. She sees me. Presses her fingers on her lips. "Oh."

"This is Iggy," Lucas says.

"Hello, Iggy. I'm cloud boy's mother." She hands him a twenty-dollar bill. "Dad and I both have shows tonight."

"Okay," he says.

She winks at me. "You're welcome to stay." On top of everything else, she has a big smile. And very white teeth. She closes the door.

"Your mom is really pretty," I say.

"She's a dancer. At the Bellagio casino."

"Really? Wow."

"Wow what?" he asks.

"I don't know. I thought your parents would be … different. Librarians or teachers or something."

He shrugs.

I look at the twenty in his hand. "What's that for?"

"Pizza for me and Cleo."

"Who's Cleo?" I ask.

"My little sister."

His sister. The sister with the puppy! I'd almost forgotten. "I should probably see the puppy now. My dad will freak if I don't get home soon."

He leads me to a very pink bedroom. *Frozen* bedspread, curtains, and pillows. A black furball bounds into the room. Skids into my ankle. It rolls onto its side. Staggers to its feet. And looks up at me.

There is nothing—*nothing*—on this planet cuter than this dog.

"His name is Doc," Lucas says. "He's a Labradoodle."

I pick him up. His fur is fluffy-feather soft. He squirms. Licks my nose. His little heart flutters against my hands.

"Hey! That's my dog." A frowning redheaded girl glares up at me.

"Oh. Sorry." I hand Doc to her. "Your puppy is really cute."

"Who are *you*?"

"This is Iggy," Lucas tells her. "A friend of mine."

"You don't have any friends." She says it like she's stating a fact. Not trying to be mean.

He sighs. "Do you want pepperoni, Hawaiian, or the Works?"

"Hawaiian."

"Have you seen enough of the puppy?" he asks me.

"Sure." Of course I haven't. I could hold that puppy all day.

"Do you want to stay for pizza?" he asks hopefully.

"No. I really have to get home."

He leads me through the living room. His dad meets us at the front door. "Iggy, angel," he says.

"Leaving so soon?" He bursts into a song. This one about loving me tender.

He has a good voice. But I'm about to die of embarrassment.

Lucas just shrugs. He smiles like this happens all the time.

"Well, I'd better go," I say when he finishes singing. "Thanks for the song, Mr. Elvis."

"Well, thank you," he croons. "Thank you very much. Hold on a sec, darlin'." He leans over. Whispers to Lucas. Lucas smiles and nods. Mr. Elvis pats Lucas's shoulder. Then he winks and walks away humming.

Lucas takes a deep breath. "Would you like to see my dad's show? On New Year's Eve? It's at the Lucky Gold Casino. He can get us in for free. But I understand if you can't. It's totally okay."

"A real casino? On the Strip?"

He nods. "Dad will drive us."

My stomach backflips. Part of my brain knows the wannabe weatherman thinks he's asking me on a date. But the rest of my brain doesn't care. "Well, yeah! Of course!"

"Really?" He grins. "Do you need to check with your parents first?"

"Oh, right."

"You can call me when you find out."

"Okay." We exchange numbers.

I skip down the walkway. Run all the way home.

Finally.

Vegas, baby!

CHAPTER 7

HONESTY CODE

Dad and I go to the movie. It's one I've wanted to see. It's pretty funny. But I keep thinking about how to get his permission to go to Mr. Elvis's show. I finally build up my courage. After dinner I explain everything while we're washing dishes.

He stops rinsing the frying pan. Stares at me. "So these past few afternoons. When we thought you were walking around the block. You were going to the park? And meeting *a boy*?"

"I never actually said I was walking around the block."

"Iggy, I don't approve of this. At all. You're not to go to the park alone!"

"But Lucas is a geek. He likes swings. And clouds. His sister has a puppy. He limps!"

"I don't care—"

"His mom and dad are really nice."

"You met his parents? Where? At the park?"

"No. At their house."

"YOU WENT TO THIS BOY'S HOUSE?" He squeezes his eyes shut. Then he opens them. He says, "You are not going with these strangers into town. That's final."

I throw the dish towel on the counter. Stomp to the guest room. Slam the door. I keep thinking he'll come in. Apologize. But he doesn't.

Dad stays home over the weekend. I think so he can keep an eye on me. I don't dare sneak off to the park. I don't even go for a walk. The most fun thing we do is order pizza Saturday. Watch a DVD. I should call Lucas. Tell him I won't be going to his dad's show. But I can't bring myself to do it. It's just too sad. Plus, I still have a glimmer of hope.

I wake up Monday morning. Dad is backing his car out of the driveway. He's leaving me a prisoner on Coyote Avenue. Again. I get dressed. Take a deep breath. My last speck of hope hinges on my stepmom.

I wander into the kitchen. Tiffany is sitting at the counter. She has her laptop and a cup of coffee.

"Hi." I sit next to her.

"Good morning, Iggy."

I tap my fingers on the counter. "I think New Year's Eve is really lame. Don't you? Adults go off to parties. Kids have to stay home. It's so unfair." I try to work my face into a tragic expression. But I may just look like I'm holding back a fart.

"Your father doesn't want you seeing that boy again," she says. "And he certainly doesn't want you going to a casino on New Year's Eve."

"Okay, but—"

"He said you might try to talk me into letting you go."

Anger bubbles up fast and furious. "My vacation is almost over. I haven't done anything fun. I have this chance to see Las Vegas. With adult supervision!"

"It's not safe."

"How do you know?"

"I just do." She pauses. "And we don't know this boy or his family."

"Then meet them. Call them on the phone."

"That's not the point."

"You can't go out of your way to do this for me? You hate me that much?"

She turns white. "Your father doesn't think it's a good idea."

"But what do *you* think?"

Her eyes tear up. She gets to her feet. Trots to her office.

"You are such a wimp!" I yell after her.

I go to the guest room. Grab my hoodie. I almost slam the front door. But I close it gently at the last minute. I don't want her to know I'm leaving.

Lucas opens his front door. "Hi. I thought you were going to call."

I sigh. "I know."

His pajamas are covered with cartoon penguins.

"What, no clouds?" I ask.

He looks down at himself. Then back at me.

"Sorry," I say. "It was a bad weekend."

I follow him into the living room. He sits on the floor. Picks up a bowl of Cheerios and milk. Stares at the TV. Wind and rain blow sideways across the screen.

"I've seen this documentary a bunch of times," he says. "This is the best part."

"The Weather Channel?"

He nods.

I sit cross-legged on the floor next to him. A velvet painting of Elvis Presley hangs over the fireplace. Something cold and wet brushes my left elbow. Doc snuffles me. "Hi, Doc." I pick him up. Bury my face in his fluffy fur. He squirms. Runs off.

A small hand presses on top of my head. Cleo.

"Can we watch *Frozen?*" She sinks to the floor. Sits next to me. She's holding a box of Cocoa Crisp cereal.

"I guess," Lucas says grumpily. He gets up. Inserts a DVD into the player.

Cleo hands me the box of cereal.

"Thanks." I help myself, remembering I didn't eat breakfast.

"Good morning, Graceland!" Mr. Elvis booms.

"Lucas's girlfriend is here," Cleo says.

"Cleo, don't be a brat," Lucas says.

"I see she's here, darlin'," Mr. Elvis sing-songs. "And is Miss Iggy coming to my concert tomorrow night?"

I can't help laughing. "Um …" My stomach clenches. But I blame it on the dry cereal. "Sure."

He leaves the room singing.

Lucas smiles. "That's great your parents said okay."

"Yeah," I mutter. "Great." It's a good thing I'm not a weatherperson. No honesty code.

We watch *Frozen* until it ends. Then Lucas and I discuss New Year's Eve plans.

I only leave Lucas's house because I figure Tiffany has discovered I'm missing. She may have even called the police by now. At the very least I imagine she's standing in the doorway with her arms crossed. A rolling pin in her hand.

But she's in her office with the door closed. Most likely crying while she writes sympathy card verses.

At least that makes what I have to do next a lot easier.

CHAPTER 8

VEGAS, BABY!

It's a simple plan. I've seen it work a million times on TV.

It's New Year's Eve morning. I pretend my stomach is queasy. Then I get a headache. I cough feebly whenever Tiffany's around.

Dad gets home from work. And now I have the worst cold ever. I've scattered wadded tissues around my bed. Rubbed my nose until it's red.

Dad knocks quietly. "Iggy?" He steps inside. "Tiff says you're not feeling well."

"I have a cold," I mumble.

"I'm sorry, pumpkin." He pats my head. "It's not fun being sick. Especially on your vacation."

Some vacation, I think. "I just need to sleep."

"Sure." He kisses my cheek. Leaves.

At six forty-five I jump out of bed. Throw on my hoodie. Grab my cell phone. Then I do the pillows-under-the-blanket trick. Crawl out the window.

Mr. Elvis's show at the Lucky Gold Casino starts at nine. But we need to leave Lucas's house at seven. That's to allow time for driving. Parking. Then Mr. Elvis's costume fitting. Makeup. Voice practice. Etcetera. It all sounded very exciting when Lucas explained it to me.

I jog down Coyote Avenue. Try not to think about Dad killing me. If he finds out what I've done.

Mr. Elvis's black SUV isn't the oldie-style car I expected. It's not one of those boats on wheels with lots of chrome. But I'm grateful for the ride.

I don't complain. I climb into the backseat, and Lucas sits up front. We're only on the freeway a few minutes. Then Mr. Elvis points. He says, "Look up there, darlin'."

I perch on the edge of the backseat. Out the front windshield the sky glows. It's like an upside-down bowl of light. "Cool. That's the Strip?"

"You bet."

The lights get brighter. And brighter. Then suddenly we're on the off-ramp. And we're here! Right in the middle of the Strip! I press my nose to the window. We're driving under scads of neon. Sparkly, blinking, exploding neon. All colors and shapes. The light is so bright. I could read a book by it. But reading is the last thing on my to-do list.

Crowds flow up and down the sidewalks. In and out of casinos. Couples with their arms around each other. Groups of people. Some dressed in fancy clothes. Others in jeans and hoodies. Kids. Families. Old people.

"This is so cool!" I want to join them.

We pass by a huge fountain. A wall of water shoots up impossibly high. Then it swirls into amazing shapes. There's a huge boom sound. Down the street a pirate ship rocks on a rough sea. Smoke blows from its cannon.

I don't get Dad and Tiffany. What do they have against this city? It's the best place ever.

"Here we are, children," Mr. Elvis says.

We're passing a gold building. It's lit with a zillion round, white lights. Like someone has turned a treasure chest inside out. "Lucky Gold" flashes in huge neon letters. There are tall glass doors.

"It's beautiful," I say.

Mr. Elvis turns into a parking lot. I jump out as soon as he stops. I'm itching to join the ton of people entering the front of the casino.

"Iggy!" Lucas calls. "This way."

He and his dad are heading toward the back of the building.

I shrug. Follow them.

We stop at a small dented door. There's one lightbulb hanging above it. There's a sign. It reads Staff Only.

A private entrance. Just for casino employees. That may be even cooler than going in the front. I can hardly stand still. Mr. Elvis slides a keycard into the lock. "Welcome to the Lucky Gold Casino!" he announces.

We go through the doorway.

"You know the drill," Mr. Elvis says to Lucas. "Tell Iggy what to do."

"Sure, Dad."

The heavy metal door slams shut behind us. The electronic lock clicks into place.

Mr. Elvis leads us down a dim narrow hallway.

I poke Lucas in the back. "What was your dad talking about? What drill?"

"They don't like kids in here," he whispers. "So you need to be quiet."

"I don't get it."

"Just don't make a scene. And stay away from the gaming rooms. The casino cops think my dad is cool. But they'll bust us if anyone complains."

"You're kidding."

CHAPTER 9

SEQUIN FOREST

I see a guy the size of a minivan. He walks down the hallway toward the three of us. His tan suit barely fits his bulging biceps.

"Hey, Bob. Break a leg," he says to Mr. Elvis.

"Thank you, Drake. Thank you very much."

Drake narrows his eyes at Lucas and me. He passes us.

"Was that a casino cop?" I whisper to Lucas.

He nods.

"He told your dad to break a leg!"

"That's stage talk. It's bad luck. You don't say good luck to a performer." Then he says, "Drake isn't very friendly to kids. Too bad he's working tonight."

"Do they carry guns?"

"I don't think so."

"You don't *think* so?"

Lucas shrugs. Like it's no big deal either way.

We pass a kitchen on the left. Plates clatter and clink. It smells sour. Like old dishwater.

Mr. Elvis leads us up a stairway. Then down another long hallway.

"Holy snot!" I suck in my breath. Flatten my back against the wall.

Walking toward us is an army of women. They're wearing practically nothing. Except sparkly Victoria's Secret-type underwear. Towering high heels. And huge turquoise headdresses. They look like almost-naked giant parrots.

"Evenin', Fran," Mr. Elvis says to the lead parrot. "How did the real estate exam go?"

"I passed!" she squeals. "I'm getting my license!"

"Hey, that's super."

A blonde woman smiles at Lucas. "You a weatherman yet?"

He blushes. "Not yet."

Mr. Elvis stops in front of a door. There's a Men's Dressing Room sign on it. He and Lucas walk in.

I wait outside.

Lucas holds the door open. "Well?"

I point at the sign.

"No one cares," he says. "You'll see."

I take a deep breath. Barge in before I lose my nerve.

It's like walking into a sequin forest. The room is filled with racks of glittery pants. Shirts. Jumpsuits. Mr. Elvis sits on a padded stool. He's in front of a mirror. It's surrounded by round makeup lights. There are bottles. Brushes. Sponges. And tissues. All are scattered across the table in front of him.

"Welcome to my office," he says.

I picture my dad's gray cubicle. Then try to imagine him working here. I can't.

"This way," Lucas says.

I follow him to a far corner. He rummages through a cardboard box. "Here." He hands me a comic book. Grabs a magazine for himself. Then he jumps on a tall director's chair. "You might as well get comfortable. We're going to be here for a while."

I sit on a chair next to him. I feel like a star on a movie set. I watch as guys come and go. They're laughing and talking. They make gargling noises in their throats. Sing and hum scales. Stretch. Change into costumes. I pretend to read when they change clothes. But Lucas was right. No one seems to care I'm here.

I pull out my cell phone. Text Sophia.

IGGY: Sharing casino dressing room with naked men!!!

I put my phone away. "Are all these guys in your dad's show?"

"Uh, no. There are three theaters in the casino. My dad's show is just his band. And two backup singers."

"So how many friends have you brought here?"

He fidgets. Rolls his magazine into a tube.

"Am I the first?"

He sighs. "I don't have many friends."

I kind of get it. That nerdiness and everything. But it's still sad. Everyone deserves at least one friend. I take a good look at him. His green eyes are nice. I like his dimples.

He meets my eyes. "Are you staring at me?"

"No. Of course not." I quickly look away. Don't want him getting the wrong idea. That I like him or something.

His dad suddenly appears in front of us. It's like the velvet painting in their living room has come to life. There's some serious gel action. His thick black hair is slicked. His tight white pants flare at the bottom. The pleated bell-bottoms are huge. The shiny material is covered with sequins. There's fancy stitching.

"You kids behave yerselves, ya hear?" he says in his Elvis voice. "I'm gonna practice now. See ya later." He hands Lucas the card that unlocks the back door. Then he winks and sashays away.

"So what do we do now?" I ask.

"We have two options," Lucas says. "We can wait in the dressing room until the show starts. Or we can walk around the Strip."

"The Strip! The Strip!" I jump off the director's chair.

"There's just one problem. We're supposed to be with an adult at all times. And now we're not. So that means we have to sneak by the casino cops. To get out and back in."

"What?"

"Don't worry." Lucas smirks. "I have a plan."

CHAPTER 10

BIG TROUBLE

Lucas proceeds to describe his plan for getting us by the casino cops. "First, we need props." He goes to another part of the dressing room. Returns with two shoulder bags. "Lucky Gold Casino, Find Your Pot of Gold" is printed on the side of each bag. He hands me one. "Carry this. We'll look like performers carrying our stuff."

"Do kids perform in casino shows?" I ask.

"No, but little people do."

"You mean dwarves?"

He nods.

"I think I'm too tall. So are you."

"Then make yourself look shorter."

"Um … I'm not sure I should mention this. But what about your meteorologist's code of honesty?"

He thinks a minute. "This is playacting. Playacting isn't the same as lying."

"If you say so. Just make sure I don't get caught, okay? My dad will kill me."

"No problemo."

We leave the dressing room. Then look up and down the hallway. No dancers or casino cops in sight.

"This way." Lucas skulks down the hallway. He's a junior secret agent with a limp.

We get downstairs. So far so good. Then I see the human minivan. He's parked near the exit.

"Oh, shoot. It's Drake," Lucas whispers.

My pulse quickens. "What do we do?"

"Don't worry. I've got a plan for this too. We're going to act like we're old friends. Don't look him in the eyes. He'll see our faces. Know we're kids." Lucas reaches for me. "I'm going to touch you. But it's just playacting, okay?"

I don't have a chance to argue. He's already linking his arm through mine. He pulls me down the hallway. Then he says, "Can you believe Walt fell on his butt during that last routine? It was so comical!" He lets out a huge laugh. It sounds so fake.

I'm sure his terrible acting will catch Drake's attention. But the casino cop leans against the wall. His arms are crossed over his chest. We're as interesting as fingernail clippings to him.

We pass Drake. Reach the door. I'm just feeling hopeful. Then he says, "Hey, wait a sec."

Lucas fumbles with the door handle.

"Hold on!" Drake says.

Lucas shoves the door open. We sprint outside.

"Hey!" Drake screams at us from the doorway. "You and your dad can get in big trouble!" I expect him to chase us. But he goes back inside.

It looks like we're safe. But we don't stop

running until we reach the sidewalk in front of the casino.

"We did it!" Lucas says, gasping for breath.

"Yeah," I pant. "Except we almost got caught."

He shrugs. "I knew you really wanted to see the Strip. So is it worth it?"

I look up and down the street. The lights are super bright. Cars rev their engines and honk. People talk and laugh. I'm standing on the Las Vegas Strip. The very same Strip Tiff-Daddy refused to take me to. The one I've been trying see for two weeks. I smile at Lucas. "It's worth it. Thanks. So now what?"

"Up to you."

Someone bumps my shoulder. People are jamming their way into the casino. "I haven't been inside a casino yet. Come on."

"No." Lucas grabs my arm. "Kids aren't allowed inside. Remember?"

"I thought you said we couldn't be in the gaming rooms."

"Well, that's pretty much what a casino is. Gaming rooms."

"We're not allowed in *at all*?"

"Gambling is for adults. I thought everyone knew that."

"But I don't want to gamble. I just want to look. Crud." I press my hands on my hips. "Where's the Adventuredome?"

"About five blocks that way." He points down the street. "How much money do you have?"

"Twenty dollars."

"That'll last about a minute. It's expensive."

"What about a roller coaster?"

"That's expensive too. And crowded. The lines are long. By the time we get through it, Dad's show will be over."

"Then why did we come out here?"

"Because you wanted to see the Strip."

"Okay. So now I've seen it. There's got to be something fun to do."

Someone bumps me again. The guy's face is

shiny red. And he stinks. "You wanna do some-thin' fun?" he slurs. He looks me up and down. "You're cute, dolly. Whatchyer name?" He tries to wrap his arm around me.

"Ew. Leave me alone!" I push his arm away.

"Hey!" His face turned redder. "Dat's not nice."

Lucas slips between the two of us. "Beat it!" He puffs out his chest. Balls his hands into fists.

The drunk sneers at Lucas. "Okay. Be that way, punks." He backs up. Trips. And staggers across the street.

Lucas gently takes my hand. He leads me down the sidewalk. We move through the New Year's Eve crowd. It seems to double in size every second.

CHAPTER 11

DO WHAT I DO

Lucas keeps holding my hand. We head through the crowd. My brain screams, *Red alert! Embarrassing boy situation!* But I ignore my brain. That drunk scared me. And Lucas's hand makes me feel safe.

We turn up a side street. The crowd thins. He lets my hand go.

"Where are we going?" I ask.

"A ride."

"An amusement park ride?" I ask hopefully.

"Sort of."

We pass a few hotels. Motels. Then apartment buildings. Some small houses. It's hard to believe people live this close to the Strip. It's so loud and crazy.

Huh. Ten minutes ago I was craving loud and crazy.

We reach an expanse of grass. Walk down a curving cement path. Lucas stops. I stand next to him. Stare in disbelief. "This is your ride?"

"It's free." He sits on a swing.

I don't know. Should laugh? Or cry? So I sit on a swing and sigh.

We push off at the same time. Keep pace with each other. Even when we fly almost as high as the top bar. I have no idea how much time passes. But eventually I've had enough and stop. So does Lucas.

We sit quietly for a minute.

"You've been pretty quiet tonight," I say. "Are you working on your social skills?"

He nods. "It's hard. There are so many things

I want to tell you. But I know they're only interesting to me."

"Like what?"

"Well. For instance, did you know that gambling was legalized in Nevada in 1931? That was the same year construction began on the Hoover Dam. Vegas has over fifteen thousand miles of neon tubing. Everyone thinks the temperature here is really hot. But the annual average is just sixty-nine degrees. Did you know …?" He stops. Looks at me sheepishly. "It's your turn to talk."

"Oh. Right." I think about what to say. "I'm pretty sure I hate my stepmother. I'm not happy with my dad right now either. Honestly, my mom's been acting strange since they split up too. It's like they all wish I didn't exist. Like I'm too much trouble. I wish I had your family."

"Really?"

"You're all so different. But no one seems to care. You can just be yourselves." I look at Lucas. "Your turn."

"I never thought about my family that way." His eyes widen suddenly. "Family. Dad's show!" He looks at his watch. "It starts in ten minutes! We'll never make it."

I jump off my swing. "All I've done tonight is sit in a dressing room. Get pushed around by a drunk. And swing. We will *so* make it."

If he says something, I don't hear him. I'm already running.

It doesn't seem possible. But the sidewalks are even more crowded than before.

"What do we do about the casino cops?" I ask. We've finally reached the Lucky Gold parking lot.

"I don't know. Walk fast? Stay low?"

He unlocks the staff-only door with his dad's keycard. We rush inside. Keep our heads down. Drake must be on a break. No one yells or chases us.

We take a couple of turns I don't remember from before. Then I hear music. Laughter. Clinking glasses. We reach what looks like the back of a small stage. There's a closed curtain. Colored spotlights. On stage, Mr. Elvis swivels his hips. Grinds his teeth.

"What's wrong with your dad?" I ask.

"He's psyching up for his performance."

"It looks painful."

"This way," Lucas says. "We need to find Kai. He'll save us a seat. But only if we're there in time."

We trot down a small stairway. It's next to the stage. Stop in front of a door. Lucas presses his finger to his lips. He wants me to be quiet. Then he slowly pushes the door open.

The clinking and laughter get louder. I peek under Lucas's arm. People in nice clothes sit at small round tables. Each table is covered with a red tablecloth. And a single red candle. Servers scurry between the tables carrying drinks. I have a feeling those glasses don't hold soft drinks or juice.

Lucas waves to someone. A guy wearing a tuxedo joins us in the hallway. He closes the door behind him. "Hey, dude," the guy says to Lucas. "You're cutting it short."

"I know, Kai. Sorry."

Kai looks at me. "Does your girlfriend know what to do?"

"Um, not exactly. But Iggy is cool."

"Okay. Stay low." He opens the door.

Lucas should have corrected him. I'm not his girlfriend. But I'll let it slide for now. "What are we doing exactly?" I ask.

"Just do what I do," Lucas says.

Kai takes three steps into the room. Stands next to the table closest to the door. He casually lifts the red tablecloth a few inches.

"Now," Lucas whispers. He crouches low. Slips under the table.

Wait. What?

CHAPTER 12

TABLE URCHINS

Kai motions for me to hurry up.

I take a breath. Slip through the door. Scramble under the table next to Lucas. He pulls his knees up to his chest. I copy him.

The tablecloth lowers. Kai's shiny black shoes step away.

"Now what?" I ask.

"We lift the tablecloth. But only when the show starts."

I stare at him. The tablecloth casts a red glow

on his face. "We're going to watch your dad's show from here?"

"Shhh. Keep your voice down." Then he says, "This is a bar. Kids aren't allowed."

"Holy snot. This is ridiculous."

"The floor is carpeted. Are you worried about someone sitting at our table? Kai won't let that happen. Unless things get really crowded."

"Gee. What's the chance of things getting crowded? It's New Year's Eve." Sweat trickles down my sides. I lift the tablecloth. It's just above my eyes.

"Don't!"

"I need air!" But I see the problem now. The tables curve in the shape of the rounded stage. People at the other front row tables can see us. I drop the tablecloth.

"No one will notice us once the show starts," he says.

The lights dim. A voice booms from a microphone. "Ladies and gentlemen, the Lucky Gold

Casino is pleased to present. Straight from Graceland …" There's a loud drumroll. The voice shouts, "Mr. Elvis!"

Music blares. Someone starts singing. It must be Lucas's dad.

Lucas elbows me. Lifts his side of the tablecloth. I do the same.

The song is catchy. The crowd sings along.

I forget I'm watching a Las Vegas show from the floor of a bar. Just for a second. But it's more listening than watching. We're sitting low. I only see Lucas's dad when he lurches in our direction. The first time that happens, he points at us and winks.

Something taps the side of my foot. I look down. See black patent leather. Kai taps my foot again.

Suddenly the chairs at our table slide back. Above us Kai says, "Enjoy the show. Your server will be right with you."

"Cripes," Lucas mutters.

We both scoot forward. It must look like our tablecloth has grown two lumps. Things are going so poorly. It doesn't surprise me when something sharp jabs me in the back.

I twist around. A woman's pointy-toed shoe is a few inches from me. It starts bouncing in time to the music. Hits my ear.

"Ow!" I slap her foot.

The legs uncross. The foot slams to the floor. Manicured fingers lift the tablecloth. A woman glares at me under the table. "What the heck?"

By now Lucas is seeing what I'm seeing. "Oh no. Come on." He crawls out from under the table. I follow him.

We run to the door. Scramble through it. We just hear Mr. Elvis finish his first number. The audience claps and cheers. It could be that no one saw us escape. But I'm guessing that woman is complaining. Blah. Blah. There were urchins hiding under her table. And attacking her foot.

We're almost to the back door of the casino. I look up ahead. A guy in a tan suit guards the exit. He's talking on a cell phone. Drake.

We stop behind a tall cart near the kitchen.

"I can't get caught. Remember?" I tell Lucas.

"I know."

Drake hasn't moved. But he looks around, frowning. As if he'd like to break our legs for real.

"I have an idea," Lucas says. "This way." He slips back the way we came. Disappears around a corner.

I follow him. Go through a door into the bright lights of the casino. We hide behind a fake palm tree. I have to squint against the lights. Row after row of slot machines spread in front of us. They're like a crop of robots. Each robot has its own person-controller sitting in front of it. My eyes sting from the cigarette smoke. The machines *jangle. Jingle. Clink.* And *twitter* hysterically.

"The entrance is way on the other side," Lucas

says. "Through a couple of these gaming rooms. They build casinos like mazes. It's to keep people from leaving too easily."

"That's creepy."

"Sure is. That's what Dad says. There's a whole psychology to these places." He looks at me. "I walk slower than you. Because of my leg. If we get separated, just keep going. We'll meet at the swings."

I nod. "If there's a weather disaster? You'd be a good friend to have, Lucas."

"I know." His eyes soften. He leans in. Kisses my cheek. He could have used a breath mint. But my skin tingles just the same.

CHAPTER 13

CASINO COPS

Lucas steps quickly between the crowded slot machines.

I rub my cheek. It wasn't much of a kiss. But it's officially my first. If cheek kisses count. I'll have to think about it later. When my situation isn't so dire.

I step onto the casino floor. Start walking. No one stops us. I'm just thinking we're going to make it. Then I hear Lucas cry, "Let me go!"

A guy in a tan suit grips his shoulder.

"Run!" Lucas mouths to me.

I think about it. I really do. But he's been pretty heroic tonight. And I feel like I should return the favor. So I stay put.

"You the kids who snuck into the Elvis show?" the guy asks.

Lucas opens his mouth to answer. But nothing comes out. His code of honesty! He can't lie.

"No!" I say, thinking fast. "We're lost. Our mom is a dancer. She let us go backstage. But only for a second. She told us to go straight outside. But we got turned around. Can you take us to the main entrance? Please?" I smile sweetly.

"Right." He sneers. "What's your mom's name?"

"Fran," I say. I remember the dancer from earlier.

"Fran Kawalski is your mom?" His eyes bug out.

"Sure." I shrug.

He yanks the phone off his belt. Makes a call. "Describe those two kids again?" He stares at us. Listens to the answer. "Uh-huh. Right. Thanks." He clips the phone back on his belt. "Looks like I'm taking you both in." He reaches for me.

I kick him in the shin.

"Ow! Hey!" he shouts. I hoped he'd let Lucas go. But he holds tight.

"Run!" Lucas yells.

This time I take his advice. I run into another gaming room. The *jingle-jangle* never lets up. The noise and the cigarette fumes give me a headache. This party stinks.

I hide behind a slot machine. A shiny new car sits high up. It's on a platform above a circle of slots. Past that are the doors to the main entrance. Finally!

Two casino cops study the crowd. They're like cowboys watching cattle.

I'm the calf about to break from the herd.

My heart beats fast. My palms sweat.

Suddenly there's a humongous clanging in another part of the casino. Someone shouts joyfully. The cops look in that direction. This is my chance.

I head for the door. One of the cops sees me. "Hey!" he says. Now they're both moving toward me. The sliding door has just let in a big crowd. It's starting to close.

"Don't even think about it," the closest cop says. He reaches out to grab me.

I step right. Duck and twist. His fingers brush my arm. I shoot out the door. It shuts with a quiet *shooft*.

Yay, I did it! I escaped Crazyland Casino!

Then a meaty hand grips my arm. Drake snarls in my ear, "You're in big trouble, missy."

"Let me go." I struggle against him.

"No way. I'm turning you in."

"Get your hands off my daughter," says a familiar voice.

I turn. "Tiffany?"

She glares at Drake. Her mouth is set in a knife-thin line. "I said let her go."

"Underage gambling is a misdemeanor," he says.

"I wasn't gambling," I say.

"The casino could get a whopping fine," Drake snarls.

"I was not gambling." I pull my arm again. He grips tighter.

"She says she wasn't gambling," Tiffany says. "You're not going to charge her. So remove your hand from her arm. Now."

How does she know that? He won't charge me? Drake hesitates. Flexes his jaw. He lets me go with a little shove. Then he grins. Like he has a big secret. "You might want to ask her what she was doing in the casino in the first place."

Tiffany looks at me.

"I think I'm injured," I say. I rub my arm. Hope to change the subject.

"She snuck into a show," Drake says for me. "The Lucky Lounge. That's a twenty-one and over—"

"I know what it is," Tiffany says.

"Then you know—"

"Did she break anything? Steal anything? Was anyone hurt?"

"As a matter of fact, she slapped a woman's foot."

Tiffany doesn't even flinch. "Is this woman pressing charges?"

"Well … not that I know of."

"You don't want my daughter in the Lucky Gold Casino. Fine. From what I can see, she's not in your damned casino."

He shrugs.

Tiffany takes my hand. "Come on, Iggy."

We march down the crowded block. All I can think? *Yay, Tiffany*.

Drake's now out of her sight. Her hands start shaking. She sits on a wall next to the sidewalk. Then she bends over and cries.

CHAPTER 14

TIFF-DADDY

I sit on the wall next to Tiffany. I don't know what to do. So I pat her back. "Thanks," I say. "You were awesome."

She reaches into her purse. Her hand is still shaking. She pulls out her cell phone. Holds it out for me. I slowly take it. "C-call your dad," she says. "He's looking for you. He's frantic."

My heart shrivels. He must hate me right now. I shake my head.

"Call!" Tiffany commands.

"I can't—"

She takes the phone from me. Presses a button. "I found her," she says into it. "She's okay. We'll meet you at the car." She hangs up.

"How did you find me?" I ask.

"The GPS on your phone. We would have found you anyway. We searched online for casinos with an Elvis show." Tiffany isn't crying now. But her eyes are still red. "Iggy, you scared us to death. You have no idea how dangerous this city is for a young girl."

"It's not that bad. If it wasn't for the casino cops. And the drunks—"

Tiffany glares at me. "You have *no* idea." She wraps her arms around her stomach. Like she's trying to keep from hurling. "We'd better go. Your dad's probably at the car." She starts walking toward the parking lot behind the casino.

Tiffany is very interesting all of a sudden. But now *I* feel like hurling. I'm worried what Dad will say. And I'm worried about Lucas.

Dad runs up to us. He wraps me in a hug. "Don't you ever, *ever* do that again," he whispers into the top of my head.

Before he starts yelling, I say, "Dad, we need to help Lucas. He's in trouble with the casino cops."

Dad pushes me away. Meets my eyes. "The boy who got you into this mess? Let his father get him out of trouble."

"But Mr. Elvis's show isn't over until eleven thirty. They could be breaking Lucas's legs by now."

"Don't be ridiculous. He's a child."

"Dad, those guys are big. And mean."

Tiffany touches his arm. "I'll try."

"What?" Dad sighs. "No, you stay and I'll—"

"You don't know what to say, Carlos. I do."

Dad seems to mull several things at once. Finally he nods reluctantly. "Okay. Call me if you need help."

Tiffany looks at me. "Tell me exactly what

happened." I describe sitting under the table for Mr. Elvis's show. She cracks a small smile. But otherwise she just listens. "This won't take long." She marches toward the staff entrance.

"Hey, Tiff," I call. "The door is locked! You need a—"

She waves her hand. Like it doesn't matter.

All I can say is, "Wow."

"I'm glad you're safe," Dad says. "But I'm very disappointed."

Here it comes. "I'm sorry."

"You're grounded. For the rest of your vacation. And I'm telling your mother. She'll probably ground you too."

"Okay." I can't really argue. "So what's with Tiffany? Why did she switch from mouse to macho?"

"I guess her survival instincts switched on."

"What do you mean?"

He pauses. "You'll have to ask her. And

don't count on getting an answer. She's a very private person."

"I don't get it. Why did you marry someone like that?"

"Because I'm a private person too. Tiffany understands me in a way your mom never did."

"Tiff-Daddy," I mutter.

"What?"

"Nothing."

He leans against the car. I lean next to him. He wraps his arm around me. I feel safer than I have all night. "I love you, Dad."

He squeezes me. "I love you too. You really scared me."

"I know. I'm sorry."

Two figures walk toward us. One tall. The other limping. Tiffany marches like a warrior coming home from battle. Lucas waves and smiles when he sees me.

I scan him for bruises when he gets closer.

"Did they torture you? Or did you spill the beans?"

"Spilled the beans," he said. "I'm banned for life from the casino."

"I guess I am too."

"My dad and Kai are in trouble. But I don't think they'll lose their jobs. The casino cops like them too much. But that holding room was hot. And it smelled like dirty socks and old bologna. I'm glad your stepmom sprung me."

"Yeah," I say. "Who knew she speaks casino-cop language."

"Okay, can we get out of here now?" Dad asks.

"No," Tiffany says.

We all look at her.

"They promised to tell Lucas's father that we drove him home. But I don't trust those thugs. I want to see Mr. Elvis personally." She takes a deep breath. Like she's searching her lungs for nuggets of gold courage. "Why don't we go to the Adventuredome while we wait for his show to finish."

"Really?" I say.

"Tiff," Dad says. "I just grounded Iggy. It's been a stressful night. I don't think—"

"Please." Her eyes don't sag in the least. "Let's do this."

Yay, Tiffany.

CHAPTER 15

HAPPY NEW YEAR

I have a blast at the Adventuredome. Lucas and I play a trillion and two games. And the rides are really fun.

It's 11:45. We're back at the Lucky Gold parking lot. New Year's fireworks are already booming all over the place. They add even more sparkle to the already over-sparkled Vegas sky.

"What do you think of that color, Iggy?" Tiffany points at a fountain of fireworks. They're raining down in a shimmer of yellow-orange. "Wouldn't that be perfect for your room?"

"Yeah. It's cool."

"We'll paint when you're here this summer."

"You want me to come back?"

She nods. Then whispers, "I was a dancer. When I was much younger. Barely twenty-one."

"A show dancer?"

"No. A pole dancer. Do you know what that is?"

I shake my head.

"A stripper."

Tiffany was a stripper? No! Gross. Gross. Gross. I want to wash out my brain.

"I was young. I needed the money," she continues. "A friend convinced me dancing was safe. That I'd have a great time." She shakes her head. As if she did not have a great time in the least. "That's why I hated the Strip. Bad memories. Before tonight, I hadn't been here in years."

Now I feel even guiltier. "Sorry. I didn't mean—"

"No," she interrupts. "I'm glad, Iggy. You've done me a favor. I've finally gotten that fear out of my system. I'm not twenty-one anymore." She's quiet a moment. "Why am I telling you this? Because I don't think it's a good idea to keep secrets from each other. Now that we're a family."

"Okay. Good idea."

"There he is," Lucas says. He waves at his dad. He's jogging toward us.

Mr. Elvis keeps apologizing. He even gives Dad free passes to an upcoming show. "I've learned my lesson," he says earnestly. "No more minors!" But then he winks at me.

Horns begin honking. People start yelling. It sounds like a billion slot machines. They've all marched out of their casinos. They're *jingly-jangling* in one huge Las Vegas street party.

"Happy New Year," I yell.

Dad hugs me. "Happy New Year, Iggy.

"Happy New Year!" Tiffany chimes in with a smile.

"Did you know this is a leap year?" Lucas informs us.

Mr. Elvis starts singing about rocking around the clock.

By now Tiff-Daddy have stopped paying attention. Because they're kissing.

Ew. I feel a tingle in my stomach. I have the urge to kiss someone too. Which I do. On the lips this time. Just a peck. I probably could have used a breath mint. But I don't think Lucas minded. His dimples are smiling.

Dad and Tiffany take me to the airport on Saturday. I'm sad to leave. But it will be good to get home.

"Do you think you'll change your mind?" Tiffany asks.

"Nope. Wild Mango. Definitely." She took me to Home Depot yesterday. I picked out a bunch of paint chips. She cringed just a little at the one I chose. But she's being very brave about it.

"Okay," she says. "I'll buy two gallons. We'll be all set to paint this summer."

"Cool."

The three of us hug and cry. Then I wave goodbye to Tiff-Daddy.

In no time, I'm on the plane in my window seat. We take off. I watch below as the scenery turns from highways and houses to bare dirt. It's not Oregon. But Nevada has its good points.

Lucas is taking me hiking next summer. We'll go early so we don't fry in the sun. We're going to see all the popular spots. And he's promised to teach me a thing or two about clouds.

I can't wait. It may be my best vacation ever.

WANT TO KEEP READING?

9781680211092

Turn the page for a sneak
peek at another book in the
White Lightning series:

REBEL

CHAPTER 1

TO SEE THE WORLD

Dear Patrick,

Thank you for your letter. Your family and home in America sound very nice. I would like to visit your country one day. I would especially like to see Disneyland. And I would like to meet Mickey Mouse.

You asked me to describe my home and myself. I live in a small village in Africa. It is the dry season now. It is very dusty. In a few months the rains will come. Then the ground will turn muddy. The grass will grow. I don't like mud. But we need the grass for our cattle.

I have a mother and father. I also have three younger sisters. I have many aunts, uncles, and cousins. Two of my grandparents live in our village. Our house is round. Our roof is made of reeds. The school is square. It has a blue metal roof. It is loud when the rain falls.

My best friend is Jojo. We play soccer. Only we call it football. Do you like football? I like it. I would play it all day long if I could. But I like school too. I like learning about the world. My favorite subject is geography. I want to become a teacher one day.

I am looking forward to being your pen pal.

Sincerely,
Koji

I set my pencil down. Most of my classmates are still writing. Including Jojo. Maybe I should write more. But I read over my letter. Decide it's enough. I hope Patrick writes back. I want to learn more about his life halfway around the world. I pick up my pencil again. Write a note at the bottom of the page.

Please tell me more about your life in America.

There. Now it's enough.

"Time to finish," Mr. Wek says.

Pencils hit the desks.

"Put your letters in the envelopes you addressed," he says. "Pass them to me. I will see that they get mailed."

I watch my letter. It goes hand over hand to the front of the classroom. The beginning of its long journey. I wonder how it will travel. By plane? By boat? I wish I could travel with it.

"Get out your math books," Mr. Wek says.

A few students groan. Jojo too. They don't like math. I don't mind it. I'm going to be a teacher. So I will need to know many things.

It's the end of the day. I'm restless. Want to go outside. But I try to sit still. Don't want a scolding from Mr. Wek. Finally he says, "History exam tomorrow. You may go."

Jojo and I are the first out of our seats. "Race you home," he says.

The village is a mile north. We run the whole way. I sprint at the end. But he still beats me.

"Hah! I won!" he shouts. He throws his hands in the air. Like he's a big champion.

"I'll beat you one of these days," I tell him.

"No you won't," he says. "My legs will always be longer than yours."

"Maybe. But I'm a better footballer."

He laughs. "You are not."

"Am so." I run to our hut. Grab my football. But I don't leave quickly enough.

"Koji!" my mother says. "Change out of your

uniform. And put down that ball. I need you to fetch water."

I groan. "Why can't Onaya do it?"

"Because she's helping me cook. Go on."

I quickly change out of my yellow uniform. I grab the plastic water jug. Carry it outside.

Jojo is playing football with his brothers. I sneak up behind him. Steal the ball out from under his foot. "Hey!" he shouts.

"See?" I laugh. "I told you I'm better!"

I play with them for a few minutes. I'm still holding the water jug. I'm tempted to set it down. And really play. But I need to get going or Mama will be angry.

The pump is at the other end of the village. I pass the village leader's hut. He sits outside. A number of men sit around him. My father's there. I'm surprised to see Papa here. He's usually out with our cattle.

I leave the path. Step closer to them. One man points south. Another points west. They speak in hushed and hurried voices. The one word I hear sends a chill through me. "Soldiers."

Papa spies me. Shoos me away.